On his way home from school, the young
narrator of *The Strange Library* finds himself
wondering how taxes were collected in the
Ottoman Empire. He pops into the local
library to see if it has a book on
the subject.
This is his first mistake.

Led to a special 'reading room' in a maze
under the library by a strange old man, he
finds himself imprisoned with only a sheep
man, who makes excellent doughnuts, and
a girl, who can talk with her hands, for
company. His mother will be worrying about
why he hasn't returned in time for dinner
— and the old man seems to have an appetite
for eating small boys' brains.
How will he escape?

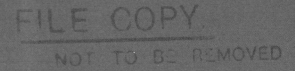

Also by Haruki Murakami

Fiction

After Dark
After the Quake
Blind Willow, Sleeping Woman
Colorless Tsukuru Tazaki and His Years of Pilgrimage
Dance Dance Dance
The Elephant Vanishes
Hard-Boiled Wonderland and the End of the World
Kafka on the Shore
Norwegian Wood
South of the Border, West of the Sun
Sputnik Sweetheart
A Wild Sheep Chase
The Wind-Up Bird Chronicle
1Q84

Non-Fiction

Underground: The Tokyo Gas Attack and the Japanese Psyche
What I Talk About When I Talk About Running: A Memoir

THE STRANGE LIBRARY

HARUKI MURAKAMI

THE STRANGE LIBRARY

———

*Translated from the Japanese
by Ted Goossen*

Harvill Secker

LONDON

Published by Harvill Secker 2014

2 4 6 8 10 9 7 5 3 1

Originally published in Japan

First published in Great Britain in 2014 by
HARVILL SECKER
20 Vauxhall Bridge Road
London SW1V 2SA

www.vintage-books.co.uk

A Penguin Random House Company

Penguin
Random House
UK

global.penguinrandomhouse.com

A CIP catalogue record for this book is available from the British Library

9781846559211 (hardback)

Penguin Random House supports the Forest Stewardship Council (FSC®), the leading
international forest certification organisation. Our books carrying the FSC® label are
printed on FSC®-certified paper. FSC® is the only forest certification scheme endorsed
by the leading environmental organisations, including Greenpeace. Our paper
procurement policy can be found at www.randomhouse.co.uk/environment

Design © Suzanne Dean

Printed and bound in Italy by Graphicom

(1)

The library was even more hushed than usual.

My new leather shoes clacked against the gray linoleum. Their hard, dry sound was unlike my normal footsteps. Every time I get new shoes, it takes me a while to get used to their noise.

A woman I'd never seen before was sitting at the circulation desk, reading a thick book. It was extraordinarily wide. She looked as if she were reading the right-hand page with her right eye, and the left-hand page with her left.

"Excuse me," I said.

She slammed the book down on her desk and peered up at me.

"I came to return these," I said, placing the books I was carrying on the counter. One was titled *How to Build a Submarine*, the other *Memoirs of a Shepherd*.

The librarian flipped their front covers back to check the due date. They weren't overdue. I'm always on time, and I never hand things in late. That's the way my mother taught me. Shepherds are the same. If they don't stick to their schedule, the sheep go completely bananas.

The librarian stamped

on the card with a flourish and resumed her reading.

"I'm looking for some books, too," I said.

"Turn right at the bottom of the stairs," she replied without looking up. "Go straight down the corridor to Room 107."

(2)

I descended a long flight of stairs, turned right, and walked along a gloomy corridor until, sure enough, I came to a door marked 107. I visited the library a lot, but the fact that it had a basement was news to me.

I knocked. It was just a normal, everyday knock, yet it sounded as if someone had whacked the gates of hell with a baseball bat. It echoed ominously in the corridor. I turned to run, but I didn't actually take a step, even though I wanted to. That wasn't the way I was raised. My mother taught me that if you knock on a door, you have to wait there until someone answers.

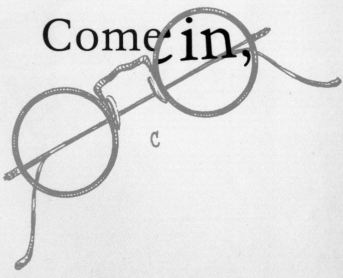

Come in,

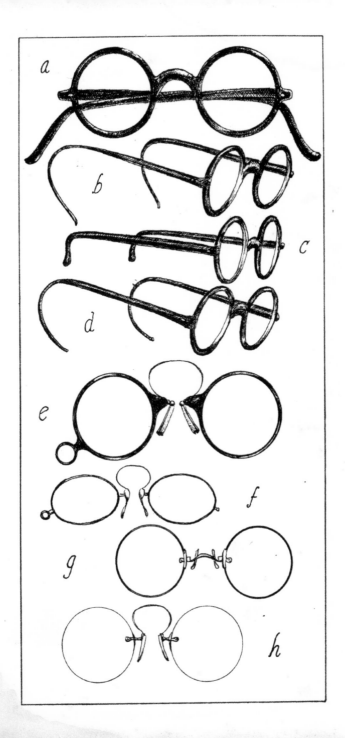

said a voice from inside. It was low but penetrating.

I opened the door.

A little old man sat behind a little old desk in the middle of the room. Tiny black spots dotted his face like a swarm of flies. The old man was bald and wore glasses with thick lenses. His baldness looked incomplete; he had frizzy white hairs plastered against both sides of his head. It looked like a mountain after a big forest fire.

"Welcome, my boy," said the old man. "How may I be of assistance?"

"I was looking for some books," I said timidly. "But I can see that you're busy. I'll come back some other time . . ."

"Nonsense, my boy," the old man replied. "This is my profession—I am never too busy! Tell me the manner of books that you seek and I will strive to locate their whereabouts."

What a funny way of talking, I thought. And his face was every bit as strange. A few long hairs sprouted from his ears. Skin dangled beneath his chin like a punctured balloon.

"And what exactly might you be seeking, my young friend?"

"I want to learn how taxes were collected in the Ottoman Empire," I said.

The old man's eyes glittered. "Ah, I see," he said. "Tax collection in the Ottoman Empire. A fascinating subject if there ever was one!"

This made me squirm. To tell the truth, I wasn't all that eager to learn about Ottoman tax collection—the topic had just popped into my head on my way home from school. As in, I wonder, how did the Ottomans collect taxes? Like that. And ever since I was little my mother had told me, if you don't know something, go to the library and look it up.

"Please don't bother," I said. "It's really not that important. It is pretty academic, after all . . ." I just wanted to get out of that creepy room as quickly as possible.

"Don't trifle with me," the old man snapped. "We possess a number of volumes that deal with tax collection in the Ottoman Empire. Did you come here with the intention of having sport with this library? Was that your aim?"

"No, sir," I sputtered. "That was not my intention at all. I wasn't trying to make fun of anyone."

"Then wait here for me like a good boy."

"Yes, sir," I replied.

The old man lurched from his chair. Back bent, he made his way to a steel door at the rear of the room, opened it, and disappeared.

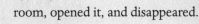

Ordo 1.st
Insecta Coleoptera
Genus I.
Scarabæi Beetles.

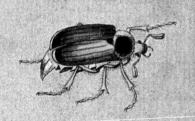

Ja.s Barbut delin.

Ja.s Nee

London, published as the Act directs Feb.y 9.th 1789, by Ja.s Barbut N.o 101 Strand.

I stood there for ten minutes, waiting for his return. Some tiny black bugs were scratching about on the underside of the lampshade.

At long last the old man returned, carrying three fat books. They were all terribly old—the smell of ancient paper rose in the air.

"Feast your eyes on these," the old man said, gloating. "We have *The Ottoman Tax System*, *The Diary of an Ottoman Tax Collector*, and *Tax Revolts and Their Suppression in the Ottoman-Turkish Empire*. An impressive collection, you must admit."

"Thank you so much," I said politely. I picked up the books and headed for the door.

"Hold your horses," the old man called out to my back. "Those three books have to be read here—under no circumstances may they leave these premises."

(4)

Sure enough, each of the books had a red label,

stuck to its spine.

"To read them you must use the inner room," the old man said.

I glanced at my watch. It was 5:20. "But the library is about to close, and my mother will be worried if I'm not home in time for dinner."

The old man's bushy eyebrows drew together in a single line. "Closing time is not a concern." He frowned. "They do what I tell them—if I say it's all right, then it's all right. The real question is, do you value my assistance or not? Why do you think I lugged these three heavy books out here? For my health?"

"I beg your pardon," I apologized. "I never intended to be such a bother. I had no idea the books couldn't be taken out."

The old man gave a rumbling cough and spat out a gob of something into a tissue. The black speckles on his face were dancing with rage.

"It doesn't matter what you did or didn't know," he snarled. "When I was your age I felt fortunate just to have the chance to read. And here you are, whining about the time and being late for dinner. What nerve!"

"All right, I'll stay and read," I said. "But just for thirty minutes." I'm not very good at giving anyone a clear no. "But I really can't stay any longer than that. When I was very small, I was bitten by a big black dog on my way home from school, and ever since then my mother starts acting strange if I'm even a little bit late."

The old man's face relaxed slightly.

"So then you'll stay and read?"

"Yes. But only for thirty minutes."

PLATE 37

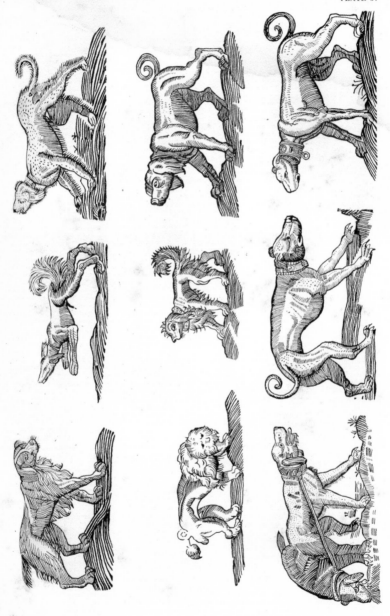

"Then please step right this way," the old man beckoned. Beyond the inner door was a shadowy corridor lit by a single flickering bulb. We stepped into the dying light.

(5)

"Just follow me," said the old man.

We had gone only a short distance when we came to a fork in the corridor. The old man turned right. A little farther on was another fork. This time he bore left. The corridor forked and forked again, branching off repeatedly, and in every case the old man chose our route without a moment's hesitation, swerving first to the right, then to the left. Sometimes he would open a door and we would enter a completely different corridor.

My mind was in turmoil. It was too weird—how could our city library have such an enormous labyrinth in its basement? I mean, public libraries like this one were always short of money, so building even the tiniest of labyrinths had to be beyond their means. I considered asking the old man about this, but I feared that he'd shout at me again.

Finally, the maze came to an end at a large steel door. Hanging on the door was a sign that read "Reading Room." The whole area was as quiet as a graveyard in the dead of night.

The old man extracted a jangling ring of keys from his pocket and chose a big old-fashioned one. He inserted it into the keyhole, shot me a brief but meaningful glance, and turned it to the right. There was a loud clunk as the bolt

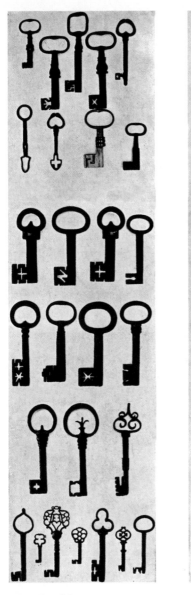 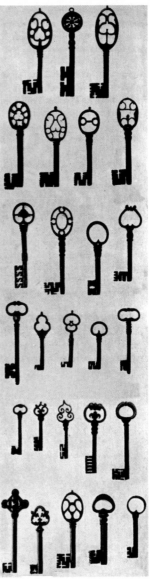

73. a. Barrel keys   *b. Keys with ornamental bows*

fell into place. The door swung open with a long and nasty screech.

"Well, well. Here we are," said the old man. "In you go."

"In there?" I asked.

"That's the idea."

"But it's pitch black,"

I protested.
Indeed,
inside the
door was as
dark as if
a hole had
been
pierced in
the
cosmos.

The old man turned to me and drew himself up to his full height. Now, suddenly, he was big. The eyes beneath the bushy eyebrows flashed like a goat's eyes at twilight.

"Are you the sort of boy who finds fault with every little thing, however trivial?"

"No, sir. I'm not like that at all. But it seems to me that—"

"Enough of your prattle," the old man said. "I cannot abide people who conjure up a raft of excuses, disparaging the efforts of those who have gone out of their way to help them. Such people are common trash."

"Please forgive me," I apologized. "I'll go in."

Why do I act like this, agreeing when I really disagree, letting people force me to do things I don't want to do?

"There's a stairway right on the other side of this door," the old man said. "Hold tight to the railing so you don't take a tumble."

I went in first, inching my way along. When the old man closed the door behind us, all went completely dark. I could hear the click as he turned the lock.

"Why did you lock the door?"

"Those are the rules. It must stay locked at all times."

What could I do? I began my descent. It was a very long staircase. Long enough, it seemed, to reach Brazil. The handrail was flaky with rust. Not a ray of light anywhere.

Finally, we reached the bottom of the staircase. I could see a glimmer farther in, just a feeble glow, really, but still strong enough to make my eyes hurt after the long darkness. Someone approached me from the back of the room and took my hand. A small man clad in the skin of a sheep.

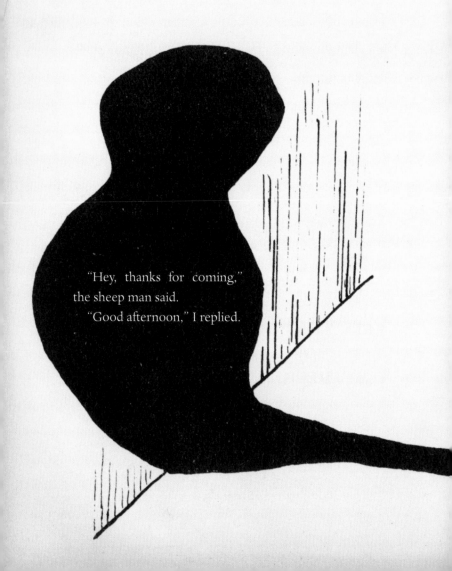

"Hey, thanks for coming," the sheep man said.

"Good afternoon," I replied.

(7)

It was a real sheepskin, and it covered every inch of the sheep man's body. There was an opening for the face, however, through which peeped a friendly pair of eyes. The costume suited him well. The sheep man looked at me for a moment; then his eyes shifted to the three books in my hand.

"Holy moly, you came here to read, for real?"

"That's right," I answered.

"You mean you *really and truly* came to read those books?"

There was something strange about the sheep man's way of speaking. I found myself at a loss for words.

"Come on, out with it," the old man demanded. "You came here to read, is that not a fact? Give him a straight answer."

"Yes. I came here to read."

"You heard him," the old man crowed.

"But, sir," said the sheep man. "He's only a kid."

"Silence!" thundered the old man. He drew a willow switch from his back pocket and whipped the sheep man across his face. "Take him to the Reading Room now!"

The sheep man looked troubled, but he took my hand anyway. The switch had left a red welt next to his lip. "Okay, let's get going."

"Where?"

"To the Reading Room. You came to read those books, didn't you?"

The sheep man led me down a narrow hallway. The old man followed close behind us. There was a short tail attached to the back of the sheep man's outfit that bounced from side to side with each step, like a pendulum.

"Well, well," said the sheep man, when we reached the end of the hallway. "Here we are."

"Just a minute, Mr. Sheep Man," I said. "Is this by any chance

A JAIL CELL ?

"Sure is," he replied.

"You hit the nail on the head," said the old man.

"This isn't what you told me," I said to the old man. "I came this far only because you told me we were going to a reading room."

"You got taken," the sheep man said and nodded.

"That's right, I pulled the wool over your eyes," said the old man.

"How could you . . ."

"Silence, you fool," the old man snarled, pulling the willow switch from his pocket and brandishing it over my head. I quickly stepped back. No way I wanted my face whipped by that thing.

"In you go—no more arguments. You will memorize those three volumes from cover to cover," the old man said. "One month from now I will personally examine you. If I conclude that you have mastered their contents completely, then I will set you free."

"It's impossible to memorize three books as thick as these," I said. "And my mother is getting pretty worried about me right about now . . ."

The old man bared his teeth and brought the switch down hard. I jumped out of the way, and the blow struck the sheep man in the face. Enraged, the old man whipped the sheep man again. It was awfully unfair.

"Throw him in the cell. I leave it to you," the old man ordered, and left.

"Are you hurt?" I asked the sheep man.

"It's okay. Hey, I'm used to it," he said. He really did seem to be all right.

"I hate to do this, but I got to lock you up."

"What if I say no, if I refuse to go in there? What happens then?"

"Then he'll hit me even harder."

I felt sorry for the sheep man, so I entered the cell. It had a simple bed, a desk, a sink, and a flush toilet. A toothbrush and a cup sat beside the sink. Neither looked what you could call clean. The toothpaste was strawberry, a flavor I can't stand. The sheep man was playing with the desk lamp, switching it on and off.

"Hey, look at this," he said, turning to me with a grin. "Pretty neat, huh?"

(9)

"I'll bring you three meals every day," said the sheep man. "And at three o'clock I'll give you doughnuts for your snack. I fry up the doughnuts myself, so they're crispy and delicious."

Fresh doughnuts are one of my all-time favorite things.

"Okay, so stick out your tootsies."

I stuck out my feet.

The sheep man pulled a heavy-looking ball and chain out from under the bed, wrapped the chain around my ankle, and locked it. He dropped the key into his breast pocket.

"It feels awfully cold," I said.

"Don't worry, you'll get used to it."

"Mr. Sheep Man, do I really have to stay here a whole month?"

PLATE VII.

FIG. 30.

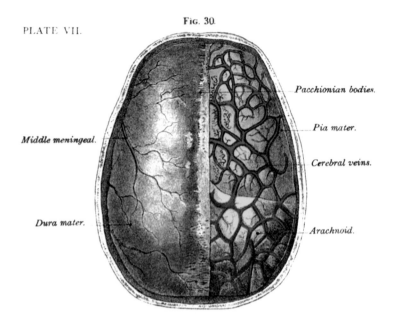

Pacchionian bodies.

Pia mater.

Middle meningeal.

Cerebral veins.

Dura mater.

Arachnoid.

FIG. 31.

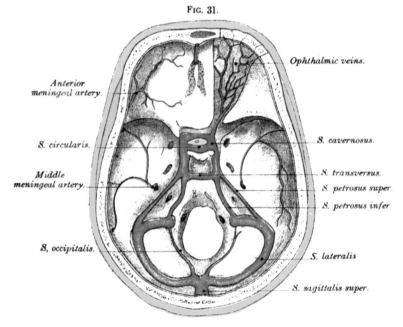

Ophthalmic veins.

Anterior
meningeal artery.

S. circularis.

S. cavernosus.

Middle
meningeal artery.

S. transversus.

S. petrosus super.

S. petrosus infer.

S, occipitalis.

S. lateralis

S. sagittalis super.

Venous Sinuses.

"Yep, that's about the size of it."

"But if I memorize everything in these books, he'll let me out, right?"

"I don't think that'll happen."

"But then what will become of me?"

The sheep man cocked his head to one side. "Man, that's a tough one."

"Please, tell me. My mother is waiting for me back home."

"Okay, kid. Then I'll give it to you straight. The top of your head'll be sawed off and all your brains'll get slurped right up."

I was too shocked for words.

"You mean," I said, when I had recovered, "you mean that old man's going to eat my brains?"

"Yep, I'm really sorry, but that's the way it has to be," the sheep man said, reluctantly.

(10)

I sat down on the bed and buried my head in my hands. Why did something like this have to happen to me? All I did was go to the library to borrow some books.

"Don't take it so hard," the sheep man consoled me. "I'll bring you some food. A nice hot meal will cheer you up."

"Mr. Sheep Man," I asked, "why would that old man want to eat my brains?"

"Because brains packed with knowledge are yummy, that's why. They're nice and creamy. And sort of grainy at the same time."

"So that's why he wants me to spend a month cramming

information in there, to suck it up afterward?"

"That's the idea."

"Don't you think that's awfully cruel?" I asked. "Speaking from the suckee's point of view, of course."

"But, hey, this kind of thing's going on in libraries everywhere, you know. More or less, that is."

This news staggered me. "In libraries everywhere?" I stammered.

"If all they did was lend out knowledge for free, what would the payoff be for them?"

"But that doesn't give them the right to saw off the tops of people's heads and eat their brains. Don't you think that's going a bit too far?"

The sheep man looked at me sadly. "You got dealt an unlucky card, that's the long and short of it. These things happen."

"But my mother's going to worry herself sick waiting for me. Can't you help me sneak out of this place?"

"No, that wouldn't work. If I did that, I'd be chucked into a jar full of hairy caterpillars. A big jar, with about ten thousand of the buggers crawling around, for three whole days."

"That's terrible," I said.

"So you see, I can't let you make a run for it, kid. I'm real sorry."

(11)

The sheep man departed, leaving me alone in the tiny cell. I threw myself facedown on the hard mattress and sobbed

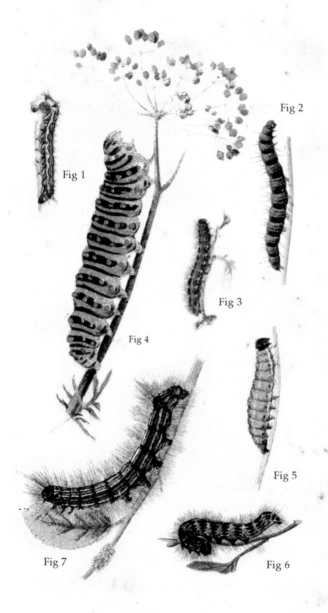

Fig 1

Fig 2

Fig 3

Fig 4

Fig 5

Fig 6

Fig 7

for one whole hour. My pillow, a blue one stuffed with buckwheat husks, was dripping wet by the end. The metal ball chained to my ankle weighed a ton.

When I checked my watch, it was exactly 6:30. My mother would be preparing dinner and waiting for my return. I could see her pacing the kitchen floor, her eyes fixed on the hands of the clock. If I still wasn't home at bedtime she might really go over the edge. That's the type of mother she is. When something happens she imagines the worst, and it snowballs from there. So she either obsesses about all the bad things that can happen or else plants herself on the sofa and stares at the TV.

At seven o'clock someone knocked on the door. A small, quiet knock.

"Come in," I said.

A key turned in the lock, and in came a girl pushing a teacart. She was so pretty that looking at her made my eyes hurt. She appeared to be about my age. Her neck, wrists, and ankles were so slender they seemed as if they might break under the slightest pressure. Her long, straight hair shone as if it were spun with jewels. She studied my face for a moment. Then she took the dishes of food that were on the teacart and arranged them on my desk, all without a word. I remained speechless, overwhelmed by her beauty.

The food looked scrumptious. There was piping-hot sea-urchin soup and grilled Spanish mackerel (with sour cream), white asparagus with sesame-seed dressing, a lettuce-and-cucumber salad, and a warm roll with a pat of butter. There was also a big glass of grape juice. When she

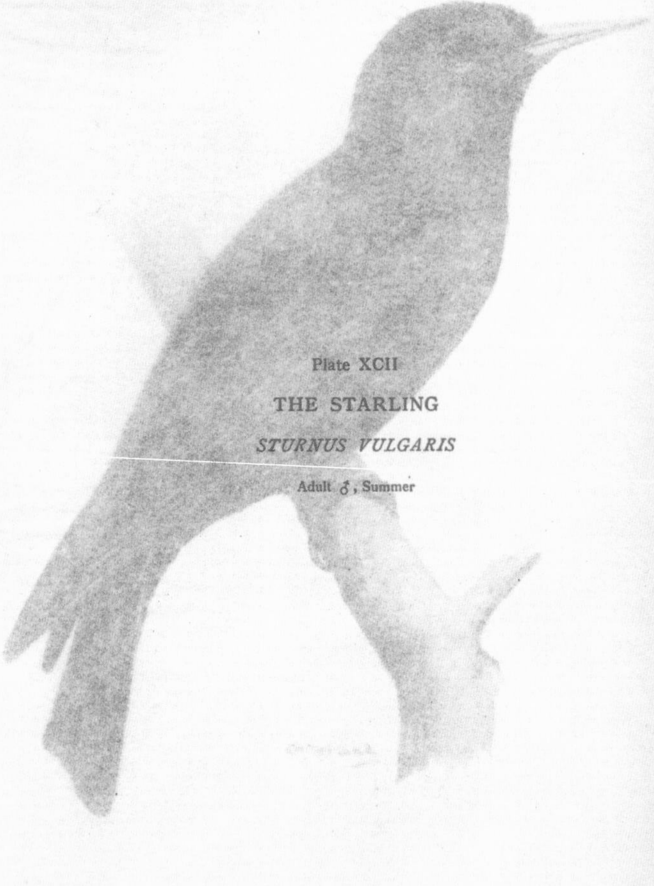

Plate XCII

THE STARLING

STURNUS VULGARIS

Adult ♂, Summer

finished laying it out, the girl turned and spoke to me with her hands: «Now wipe away your tears. It's time to eat.»

⟨12⟩

"Don't you have a voice?" I asked her.

«No, I don't. My vocal cords were destroyed when I was little.»

"Destroyed?" I cried in surprise. "By whom?"

She didn't answer. Instead, she smiled sweetly. It was a smile so radiant that the air seemed to thin around it.

«Please understand,» she said. «The sheep man isn't bad. He has a kind heart. But the old man terrifies him.»

"I understand," I said. "But still . . ."

She drew near me and placed her hand on mine. It was a small, soft hand. I thought my heart might break in two.

«Eat it while it's hot,» she said. «Hot food will give you strength.»

She opened the door and left the room, pushing the teacart in front of her. Her movements were as quick and light as a May breeze.

The food was delicious, but I could manage to get only half of it down. If I didn't make it home, the worry might drive my mother to another breakdown. She would probably forget to feed my pet starling, and it would starve to death.

Yet how could I escape? A heavy ball and chain was attached to my ankle, and the door was locked. Even if I managed to open the door, could I make it through that long maze of corridors? I sighed and started to cry again. But curling up

in bed and sniveling wasn't going to help, so I pulled myself together and finished my meal.

(13)

I decided the best thing I could do was sit at the desk and read. If I was going to find a way to escape, first I'd have to put my enemy off his guard. That meant pretending to follow his orders. I figured that wouldn't be so hard. After all, I was the type of boy who naturally followed orders.

I picked up *The Diary of an Ottoman Tax Collector* and began to read. The book was written in classical Turkish; yet, strangely, I found it easy to understand. Not only that, but each page stuck in my memory, word for word. For some reason or other, my brain was sopping up everything that I read. As I flipped the pages, I became the Turkish tax collector Ibn Armut Hasir, who walked the streets of Istanbul with a scimitar at his waist, collecting taxes. The air was filled with the scent of fruit and chickens, tobacco and coffee; it hung heavily over the city, like a stagnant river. Hawkers squatted along the streets, shouting out their wares: dates, Turkish oranges, and the like. Hasir was a quiet, relaxed sort of fellow, with three wives and six children. He also had a pet parakeet every bit as cute as my starling.

A little after nine o'clock, the sheep man showed up at my door with cocoa and cookies.

"Well, aren't you something!" he said. "But, hey, how about taking a break for some hot cocoa?"

I put down the book and helped myself to the cocoa and cookies.

"Hey, Mr. Sheep Man," I said. "Who was the pretty girl that came by a while ago?"

"Come again? What pretty girl?"

"The one who brought me dinner."

"That's weird," the sheep man said with a quizzical look. "I brought you dinner. You were lying on your bed, sobbing in your sleep. And as you can see, I'm no pretty girl, just a sheep man."

Could I have been dreaming?

CH. BROOMFIELD SULTAN

CH. RAZZLE

CH DAISY

Photo by S. O'Connor Ottawa, Ont.
PEGGIE

WALKDEN DUKE

CH. PERFECTO

Photo by S. J. Jarvis, Ottawa, Ont.
TOPSY

CH. MEERSBROOK MAIDEN

Yet the very next evening, the mystery girl showed up again. This time she brought Toulouse sausage with potato salad, stuffed snapper, radish-sprout salad, a large croissant, and black tea sweetened with honey. Just looking at all of it made me hungry.

«Take your time. Be sure to eat everything!» the girl said with her hands.

"Please, tell me who you are," I said.

«I am me, that's all.»

"But the sheep man said you didn't exist. And besides—"

The girl raised a finger to her tiny lips. I held my tongue.

«The sheep man has his world. I have mine. And you have yours, too. Am I right?»

"That you are."

«So just because I don't exist in the sheep man's world, it doesn't mean that I don't exist at all.»

"I get it," I said. "Our worlds are all jumbled together— your world, my world, the sheep man's world. Sometimes they overlap and sometimes they don't. That's what you mean, right?"

She gave two small nods.

I'm not a complete idiot. But my mind got scrambled when that big black dog bit me, and it hasn't been quite right since.

The girl perched on the bed and watched as I sat at the desk and ate my dinner. Her small hands were clasped primly on her knees. She looked like a delicate glass figurine absorbing the rays of the morning sun.

"I'd really like to introduce you to my mother and my pet starling," I said to the girl. "My starling is so smart, and very cute."

The girl tilted her head just a bit to one side.

"My mother's nice, too. But she worries about me too much. That's because a dog bit me when I was little."

«What kind of dog?»

"A big black one. It had a leather collar studded with jewels, and green eyes, and huge legs, and six claws on each paw. The tips of its ears were split in two, and its nose was reddish brown, like it was sunburned. Have you ever been bitten by a dog?"

«No, I haven't,» said the girl. «Now forget about the dog and finish your dinner.»

I stopped talking and finished my meal. Then I drank the honeyed tea. That made me nice and warm.

"I've got to escape from this place," I said. "My mother's worried, and my starling will starve if I don't feed her."

«Will you take me with you?»

"Of course," I replied. "But I'm not sure if I can make it out. I've got an iron ball chained to my ankle, and the corridor is a labyrinth. And the sheep man will receive a horrible punishment when the old man discovers I'm gone. For letting me get away."

«We can take the sheep man with us. The three of us can escape together.»

"Do you think he'll join us?"

Fig. 22.—Feathers illustrating conditions where barbicels are unnecessary and are hence reduced or entirely lost, causing downiness. 3/5 natural size.

(a) Primary of Pigeon—an important flight-feather; hence possessing a stiff vane. (b) Under wing-covert of a Great Blue Heron; downy portion was overlapped by the adjoining feather. (c) Wing-covert of Owl; the downy edge makes possible the all-important noiseless flight of this bird. (d) Feather of Ostrich; the power of flight being lost, the feathers are downy throughout the entire vane.

The girl gave me a bright smile.

Then, just like the previous evening, she slipped nimbly through the crack in the barely open door and was gone.

(16)

I was reading at my desk when I heard the sound of the lock turning, and the sheep man entered with a tray of doughnuts and lemonade.

"Here are the doughnuts I promised you earlier, straight from the pan."

"Thank you, Mr. Sheep Man."

I shut the book and took a quick bite of one of the doughnuts. It was absolutely delicious, crispy on the outside, the inside so soft it melted in my mouth.

"This is the best doughnut I've ever eaten," I said.

"I just finished frying them up," said the sheep man. "I make them from scratch, you know."

"I bet if you opened a doughnut shop, it'd be a big hit."

"Yeah, I've thought about that myself. How great that'd be."

"I know you could do it."

"But who would like me enough to come to my shop? I dress funny, and then there's my teeth. I don't look after them very well."

"I'll help you," I said. "I'll sell the doughnuts, and talk to the customers, and handle the money and the advertising. I'll even do the dishes. All you have to do is work in the back making doughnuts. I'll even teach you how to brush your teeth."

"That would be terrific," said the sheep man.

When the sheep man left, I went back to my book. As before, I became Ibn Armut Hasir, the author of *The Diary of an Ottoman Tax Collector*. I walked the streets of Istanbul during the day, collecting taxes, but when evening came, I returned home to feed my parakeet. A razor-thin crescent of white moon floated in the night sky. I could hear someone playing a flute in the distance. Having lit the incense for my room, my African servant moved about, chasing away the mosquitoes with something that resembled a flyswatter.

A beautiful young girl, one of my three wives, was waiting for me in my bedroom. It was she who served me my meals each evening.

«It's a fine moon,» she said to me. «Tomorrow it will be the new moon, and the sky will be dark.»

"We must feed the parakeet," I said.

«Didn't you feed the parakeet a little while ago?» she asked.

"You're right, I did," said the me that was Ibn Armut Hasir.

The girl's silken body glinted in the light of the razor-thin crescent moon. I was spellbound.

«It's a fine moon,» she repeated. «The new moon will shape our destinies.»

"That would be terrific," I said.

PLATE XVI

1

2

3

4

5

6

7

8

SIX INCHES

0   3   6

0   50   100   150

150 mm.

PLATE VI.

THE PHASES OF THE MOON.

Like a blind dolphin, the night of the new moon silently drew near.

The old man came to check on me that evening. He was delighted to find me lost in my book. Seeing how happy he was made me feel a little happier. No matter what the situation may be, I still take pleasure in witnessing the joy of others.

"I've got to give you credit," he said, scratching his jaw. "You've made far more headway than I anticipated. You're quite a boy."

"Thank you, sir," I replied. I do love being praised.

"The sooner you finish committing those books to memory, the sooner you can leave," the old man said to me. He raised one finger in the air. "Understood?"

"Yes," I said.

"Is anything bothering you?"

"Yes," I said. "Can you tell me if my mother and my pet starling are all right? That's got me very worried."

The old man frowned. "The world follows its own course," he said. "Each possesses his own thoughts, each treads his own path. So it is with your mother, and so it is with your starling. As it is with everyone. The world follows its own course."

I had no idea what he was talking about, but I dutifully said "yes" when he had finished.

The girl appeared not long after the old man had left. As always, she slipped in through the crack in the door.

"It's the night of the new moon," I said.

The girl sat down quietly on the bed. She seemed exhausted. She had lost her color and had grown transparent, so that I could see the wall behind her.

«It's because of the new moon,» she said. «It robs us of so much.»

"All it does to me is make my eyes sting a little."

The girl looked at me and nodded. «The moon doesn't affect you. So you will be all right. I'm sure you will be able to find a way out.»

"And you?"

«Don't worry about me. It doesn't look as though we can make it out together, but I'm sure I can join you later.»

"But how can I find my way back without you?"

She didn't answer. Instead, she came close and planted a small kiss on my cheek. Then she slipped through the door and vanished. I sat there on the bed, dazed, for a long time. The kiss had shaken me up so much I couldn't think straight. At the same time, my anxiety had turned into an anxiety quite lacking in anxiousness. And any anxiety that is not especially anxious is, in the end, an anxiety hardly worth mentioning.

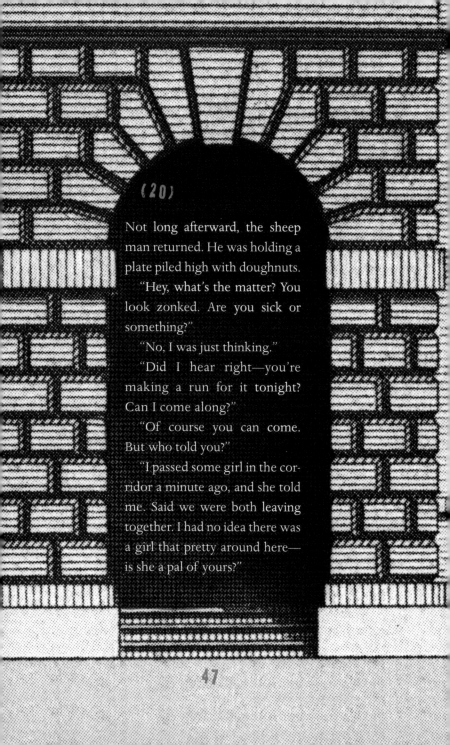

(20)

Not long afterward, the sheep man returned. He was holding a plate piled high with doughnuts.

"Hey, what's the matter? You look zonked. Are you sick or something?"

"No, I was just thinking."

"Did I hear right—you're making a run for it tonight? Can I come along?"

"Of course you can come. But who told you?"

"I passed some girl in the corridor a minute ago, and she told me. Said we were both leaving together. I had no idea there was a girl that pretty around here—is she a pal of yours?"

"Well, um . . ." I stammered.

"I see. Gosh, it would be great to have someone cool like that for a pal."

"If we can get out of here, Mr. Sheep Man, I bet you'll have lots of cool friends."

"That would be terrific," said the sheep man. "But if we don't make it out, there will be hell to pay for both of us."

"By 'hell to pay,' you mean the jar of ten thousand caterpillars?"

"That's about the size of it," the sheep man said mournfully.

The thought of sharing a jar with ten thousand caterpillars for three days sent a chill up my spine. Yet the warmth of the fresh doughnuts in my belly and the girl's kiss on my cheek had dispelled all my fears. I put away three doughnuts and the sheep man had six.

"I'm a lost cause on an empty stomach," the sheep man said, by way of apology. He wiped some sugar from the corner of his mouth with a stubby finger.

(21)

Somewhere a clock struck nine. The sheep man stood up and shook his sleeves several times to reacquaint the sheep costume with his body. It was time for us to leave. He removed the ball and chain from my ankle.

We exited the room and set off down the dim corridor. My feet were bare, for I had left my shoes in the cell. My mother would hit the roof when she learned I'd left them somewhere. They were very good leather shoes, and she had given them to me as a birthday present. Still, it wasn't worth

Fig 1

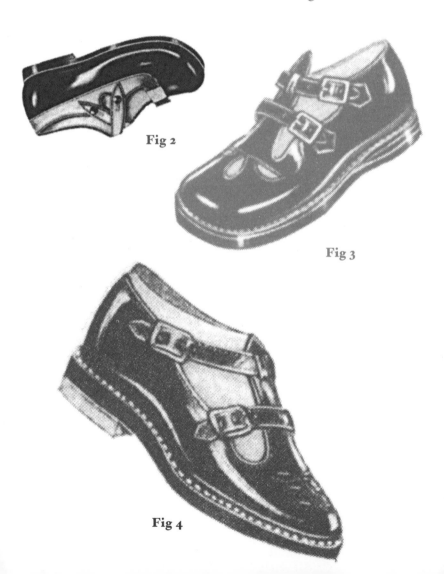

Fig 2

Fig 3

Fig 4

risking the chance that their noise might wake up the old man.

I thought about those shoes as we walked to the big metal door. The sheep man was leading the way. I was half a head taller, so his two ears were bobbing up and down right in front of my nose the whole time.

"Hey, Mr. Sheep Man," I whispered to him.

"What?" he whispered back.

"How good is the old man's hearing?"

"Tonight's the new moon, so he'll be fast asleep in his room. But he's a sharp cookie, as you've seen. So you'd best forget those shoes. Shoes you can replace, but you can't replace your brains or your life."

"You're right about that, Mr. Sheep Man."

"If he wakes up and comes after me with that willow switch, it's curtains. I'm no good to you then. When he whips me, I'm helpless—it's like I become his slave."

"Does the switch have some special power?"

"You've got me," said the sheep man. He thought for a moment. "It seems to be a pretty regular willow switch. But I don't know."

(22)

"But when he starts hitting you with it, you're helpless, right?"

"That's the size of it. So you'd best forget those shoes."

"I'll put them out of my mind," I said.

We walked a little farther down the long corridor without speaking.

"Hey," said the sheep man.

"What is it?"

"You forgot the shoes, didn't you?"

"Yes, I've forgotten them," I replied. Thanks to his question, however, the shoes that I had managed to forget walked right back into my mind.

The staircase was cold and slippery, the front edges of the stone steps worn round with use. Every so often I stepped on what felt like a bug. When you're climbing barefoot in the pitch dark, that's not a great feeling. Sometimes the thing was soft and squishy, sometimes it crunched. *Darn*, I thought, *I should have worn those shoes after all.*

At long last we reached the top of the staircase and arrived at the metal door. The sheep man pulled a large ring of keys from his pocket.

"Got to do this quietly. Don't want to wake up the old man."

"That's right," I said.

He inserted a key and turned it to the left. There was a loud "kachunk," and the door opened with a long screech. Nothing quiet about it at all.

"From here on it's a really complicated maze," I said.

"You're right," said the sheep man. "There is a maze, now that I think of it. Can't remember it too well, but we'll figure something out."

Hearing that made me a little uneasy. The tricky thing about mazes is that you don't know if you've chosen the right path until the very end. If it turns out you were wrong, it's usually too late to go back and start again. That's the problem with mazes.

As I expected, the sheep man had to try a number of routes and retreat a number of times. Yet I could feel that, somehow, we were getting closer and closer to our destination. Sometimes he would stop to run his finger along the wall and lick it with a look of great concentration. Or squat to press his ear against the floor. Or converse in undertones with the spiders who built their webs along the ceiling. Faced with intersecting paths, he might spin in place, like a whirlwind, before choosing which one he would take. Such was the manner in which the sheep man recalled the route through the maze. A far cry from the way most people would remember.

All the while, time marched on. Dawn was drawing near, and the pitch-black night of the new moon seemed to be softening bit by bit. The sheep man and I hurried along. We knew we had to reach the last door before daylight. Otherwise, the old man would wake to find us gone and would set off in pursuit.

"Think we can make it?" I asked.

"Yeah, it's looking good. From here on out, it's a piece of cake."

It was clear that the sheep man knew the rest of the way. We raced down the corridors, turning first one way, then the other, without pause. Finally, the last corridor lay dead ahead. We could see a door at the end, and light leaking through its cracks.

"See, I told you," the sheep man said proudly. "I had it figured out all along. All we have to do now is go through this door. Then you and I will be free."

1

5

7

10

15

He opened the door and there was the old man, waiting for us.

25

30

1   6

35

It was the same room where I had first met him. Room 107, in the basement of the library. He sat there in front of his desk, his eyes fixed on me.

Next to the old man sat a big black dog. A dog with green eyes and a jewel-encrusted collar. He had massive legs, and six claws on each paw. His ears forked at the tips, and his nose was a reddish-brown sunburned color. It was the same dog

who had bitten me so many years before. My pet starling's
bloody body was clamped between his teeth.

I let out a small cry and started to collapse backward, but
the sheep man caught me.

"We've been waiting and waiting," the old man said. "What took you so long? Eh?"

"I can explain everything, sir," began the sheep man.

"Silence, you fool," thundered the old man. He pulled the willow switch from his back pocket and whipped it against the desk. The dog pricked up his ears, and the sheep man fell silent. The room grew deathly still.

"Now, then," said the old man. "How shall I dispose of the two of you?"

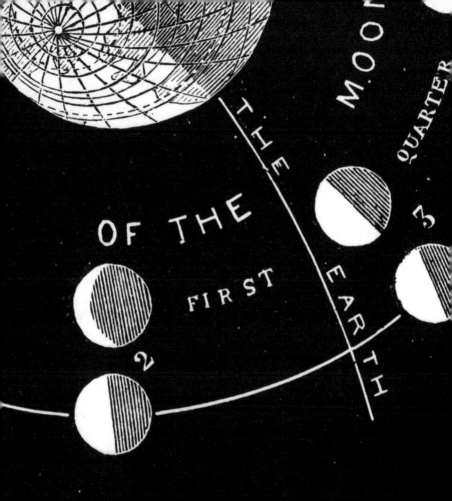

"So you weren't fast asleep, with the new moon and all?"
I asked timidly.

"You're a cheeky one, aren't you," the old man sneered. "I
don't know where you obtain your information, but I'm not
so easy to fool. I can read the two of you as easily as I can a
watermelon patch in broad daylight."

The room went black before my eyes.

My
carelessness had
ruined everything—even my pet
starling had been sacrificed. I had lost my good
shoes, and I would never see my mother again.

"And you," said the old man, pointing his switch straight at the sheep man. "I'm going to slice you up nice and fine and feed you to the centipedes."

The sheep man hid behind me, trembling from head to foot.

(25)

"As for you, my young friend," the old man said, pointing at me, "I'll feed you to this dog. He'll devour you alive. It will be a slow death. You'll die screaming. But your brains are mine. They won't be as creamy as they would have been if you had finished those books, but I'm not picky. I'll suck up every last drop."

The old man bared his teeth in a wicked smile. The dog's green eyes glittered with excitement.

It was then that I realized that the starling between the dog's teeth was growing. When it reached the size of a chicken, it forced the dog's jaws open like a car jack. The dog tried to howl, but it was too late. The dog's mouth ripped—there was the sound of shattering bones. The old man frantically whipped the starling with his willow switch. But the bird's body continued to swell until it was the size of a bull, pressing the old man fast against the wall. The small room filled with the sound of powerful wings.

R

«Run. Now is your chance,» said the starling. It was the voice of the girl.

"But what about you?" I asked the starling-who-was-the-girl.

«Don't worry about me. I'll follow later.

Qui
now

«If you don't hurry, you'll be lost for eternity,» said the girl-who-was-a-starling.

I did as she said. Grabbing the sheep man's hand, I ran from the room. I never looked back.

cK,

N° 2164. f 3.50.

N° 2163. f 3.50.

It was early morning, and the library was deserted. We raced up the stairs and across the main hall to the Reading Room, forced open a window, and tumbled out. Then we ran as fast as we could to the park, where we collapsed on the lawn. We lay there, gasping for air with our eyes closed. I didn't open mine for quite some time.

When I did, the sheep man was gone. I stood up and looked around. I called his name at the top of my lungs. But there was no reply. The morning sun was casting its first rays against the leaves of the trees. The sheep man had disappeared without a word to me. Just as the morning dew had evaporated.

(26)

My mother had set a hot breakfast on the table and was waiting for me when I got home. She didn't ask me a thing. Not about why I hadn't come home from school, or where I had spent the last three nights, or why I was shoeless—not a single question or complaint. It wasn't like her at all.

My pet starling was gone. Only its empty cage remained. I didn't ask what happened. It seemed best to avoid that topic altogether. My mother's profile seemed to have darkened very slightly, as if shadows were gathering around her. But that may have been no more than my impression.

Length, 9½in. ; depth, 7in. ; height, 15in.

FIG. 16. SHOW-CAGE.

NEST   NEST BOX

FIG. 14. SCOTCH FANCY SHOW-CAGE.

After that, I never visited the city library again.

I knew I should seek out one of the big shots who ran the place to explain what had happened to me, and to tell him about the cell-like room hidden deep in the basement. Otherwise, another child might have to endure the awful experience that I went through. Nevertheless, the mere sight of the library building at dusk was enough to stop me in my tracks.

I do occasionally think about the new leather shoes I left behind in the basement, though. That leads me to memories of the sheep man and the beautiful voiceless girl. Did they really exist? How much of what I remember really happened? To be honest, I can't be certain. All I know for sure is that I lost my shoes and my pet starling.

My mother died last Tuesday. She had been suffering from a mysterious illness, and that morning she quietly slipped away. There was a simple funeral, and now I am totally alone.

No
mother.
No pet
starling.
No sheep
man.
No girl.

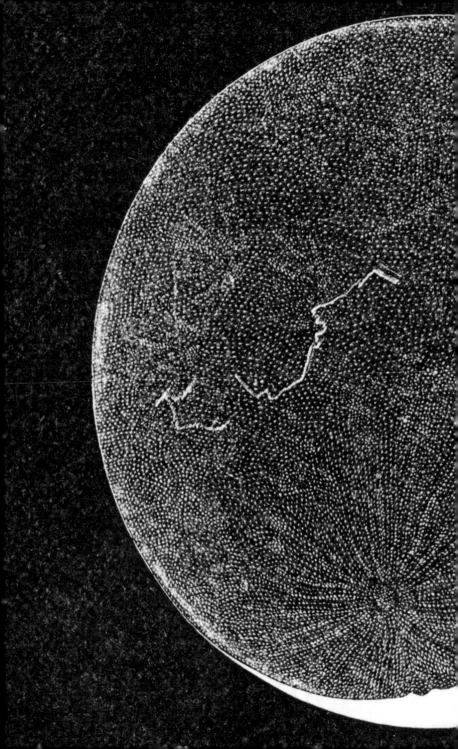

I lie here by myself in
the dark at two o'clock
in the morning and

think about that cell in the library basement. About how it feels to be alone, and the depth of the darkness surrounding me. Darkness as pitch black as the night of the new moon.

Picture Acknowledgments

Most of the illustrations in this book including marbled papers and old pages come from old books found in the The London Library, and we gratefully thank them for the rich treasury they provide.

The following sources also kindly supplied illustrations:

Bridgeman Images: pp. 34–35

Mary Evans Picture Library/Imagno: pp. 2–3, 54–55, 70–71, 76–77

Poppy Sturley: pp. 23, 41

Wellcome Library, London: pp. 8, 50–51, 52